The Truth about Hansel and Gretel

First published in 2002 by
Franklin Watts
96 Leonard Street
London
EC2A 4XD

Franklin Watts Australia
56 O'Riordan Street
Alexandria
NSW 2015

A CIP catalogue record for this book is available
from the British Library.

ISBN 0 7496 4701 9 (hbk)
ISBN 0 7496 4708 6 (pbk)

Series Editor: Jackie Hamley
Series Advisor: Dr Barrie Wade
Cover Design: Jason Anscomb
Design: Peter Scoulding

Printed in Hong Kong

The Truth about
Hansel
and Gretel

by Karina Law and Elke Counsell

W
FRANKLIN WATTS
LONDON•SYDNEY

This is my house. Isn't it beautiful?
The walls are made of gingerbread
and the roof is made of toffee.

I decorated it myself with all my
favourite sweets.

I suppose you have read the stories about me. They are all untrue, you know. I'm not really a witch. I'm just a harmless old lady.

Once upon a time, I was very happy, living in my beautiful house in the woods.

Then those dreadful children came along and spoiled everything.

I spotted them from my window.

Hansel and Gretel were their names.

I don't get many visitors so I was
going to invite them in for a nice
cup of tea.

Imagine how cross I was when I
opened the door to find them
eating my beautiful house!

My new sugar windows had just been fitted and that naughty boy was snapping off part of a peppermint window frame.

His nasty sister was licking one of
the strawberry lollipops on my
wall. What a pest!

I shouted at them to stop, and do you know what those rude children did?

They yelled, "Leave us alone, you old witch!"

As you can imagine, I was really cross and I started telling off those naughty children.

But they just sniggered and ran
straight past me into my house!

You won't believe what happened next. I followed the children into the house and, just as I was asking where they lived, that wicked boy pushed me into the oven!

His horrid sister was no better. The dreadful pair ran away, laughing.

I was left with my head stuck in a
pot of stew!

Then, to make matters worse,
those awful children told terrible
lies about me. The shame of it!

Hansel told people that I locked
him up. What a story!

And Gretel said that I was a witch who liked eating children. What a wicked thing to say!

Life has never been the same since the stories about me were printed in the local newspaper.

I don't get any visitors now.

People are afraid of me.

After all the dreadful stories
Hansel and Gretel told, people
think I'm a witch.

But you can see I'm not. Can't you?

Hopscotch has been specially designed to fit the requirements of the National Literacy Strategy. It offers real books by top authors and illustrators for children developing their reading skills.

There are 12 Hopscotch stories to choose from:

Marvin, the Blue Pig
Written by Karen Wallace, illustrated by Lisa Williams

0 7496 4473 7 (hbk)
0 7496 4619 5 (pbk)

Plip and Plop
Written by Penny Dolan, illustrated by Lisa Smith

0 7496 4474 5 (hbk)
0 7496 4620 9 (pbk)

The Queen's Dragon
Written by Anne Cassidy, illustrated by Gwyneth Williamson

0 7496 4472 9 (hbk)
0 7496 4618 7 (pbk)

Flora McQuack
Written by Penny Dolan, illustrated by Kay Widdowson

0 7496 4475 3 (hbk)
0 7496 4621 7 (pbk)

Willie the Whale
Written by Joy Oades, illustrated by Barbara Vagnozzi

0 7496 4477 X (hbk)
0 7496 4623 3 (pbk)

Naughty Nancy
Written by Anne Cassidy, illustrated by Desideria Guicciardini

0 7496 4476 1 (hbk)
0 7496 4622 5 (pbk)

Run!
Written by Sue Ferraby, illustrated by Fabiano Fiorin

0 7496 4698 5 (hbk)
0 7496 4705 1 (pbk)

The Playground Snake
Written by Brian Moses, illustrated by David Mostyn

0 7496 4699 3 (hbk)
0 7496 4706 X (pbk)

"Sausages!"
Written by Anne Adeney, illustrated by Roger Fereday

0 7496 4700 0 (hbk)
0 7496 4707 8 (pbk)

The Truth about Hansel and Gretel
Written by Karina Law, illustrated by Elke Counsell

0 7496 4701 9 (hbk)
0 7496 4708 6 (pbk)

Pippin's Big Jump
Written by Hilary Robinson, illustrated by Sarah Warburton

0 7496 4703 5 (hbk)
0 7496 4710 8 (pbk)

Whose Birthday Is It?
Written by Sherryl Clark, illustrated by Jan Smith

0 7496 4702 7 (hbk)
0 7496 4709 4 (pbk)